A WOMAN IN BLOOM

Gillianne fuller

Written by: Gillianne fuller

Book cover by: Fulcar publishing

Publisher: Fulcar Publishing

ISBN#: 978-1-0688774-1-4

TABLE OF CONTENTS

DEDICATION

To all the women who have gone through menopause, are going through menopause, this story is for you, honoring your strength, resilience and grace through this profound journey. May you find comfort, understanding and solidarity in these pages.

INTRODUCTION

In the heart of Kingston, Jamaica, where the urban pulse echoes through vibrant streets, we embark on a journey with Marley—a woman navigating the complexities of modern life. This is no ordinary tale; it's a narrative that unfolds in the quiet moments of dawn and the lively beats of reggae-filled nights.

"A Woman in Bloom" invites you into Marley's world—a world where the aroma of ackee and saltfish dances through the air, and the symphony of daily routines masks the nuanced changes beneath the surface. As the leader of a thriving marketing firm, Marley grapples with the demands of a high-powered career while concealing the silent struggles of menopause.

This is a story of resilience, transformation, and the unspoken aspects of womanhood. From the corridors of corporate success to the sanctuary of a Jamaican home, Marley's journey unfolds against the backdrop of familial joy, professional triumphs, and the profound evolution poised to illuminate the power of vulnerability and connection.

Join us as "A Woman in Bloom" navigates the intricate layers beneath the vivacious exterior, revealing the strength that lies in breaking the silence surrounding the unspoken aspects of life. The journey has just begun, and Marley stands on the brink of discovering the beauty inherent in the cycles of life—a woman in bloom, ready to embrace the transformative power of her own story.

CHAPTER 1:
A WOMAN IN BLOOM

Marley Simpson, at 45, was a force of nature in the bustling streets of Kingston, Jamaica. Her vibrant spirit radiated from the colorful patterns of her dresses, echoing the lively beat of reggae that seemed to accompany her every step. With a crown of tightly coiled curls and an air of confidence, Marley was a woman who navigated life with purpose.

As the sun dipped below the horizon, casting hues of orange and pink across the Jamaican sky, Marley would often find herself reflecting on the journey that led her to this point. A devoted mother of three, her laughter echoed through the walls of a cozy home nestled in the heart of Kingston.

Her career as an executive in a prestigious marketing firm was a testament to her tenacity. Marley had climbed the corporate ladder with determination, breaking barriers in a field where diversity was still a work in progress. A woman of eloquence, she could command a boardroom with the same grace she used to comfort her children after a stormy night.

Despite the challenges, Marley wore her achievements like a badge of honor. Her resilience was not just a personal trait but a gift she passed on to her children. Her eldest, Malik, was a university student studying engineering. The twins, Aria and Liam, added a symphony of youthful energy to their home.

In her prime, Marley reveled in the harmonious melody of family and career. Yet, as the years advanced, a subtle shift occurred beneath the surface. The invincible Marley began grappling with the unfamiliar territory of menopause. Nights of uninterrupted sleep became a distant memory as hot flashes disrupted her dreams. Fatigue lingered like an unwelcome guest, and mood swings turned the once-stable ground beneath her into a precarious terrain.

Marley's external façade remained unyielding. She continued to lead at work, a beacon of professionalism. At home, she effortlessly juggled the responsibilities of motherhood, concealing the internal tempest she faced. The vibrant colors of her dresses now masked the subtle stains of sweat caused by hot flashes.

As Marley navigated the demands of a high-powered career and the nuances of parenting, the unspoken whispers of hormonal changes intensified. Yet, admitting vulnerability was a daunting prospect for a woman who had overcome countless obstacles. The strength that defined her also became a barrier, concealing the very essence of her humanity.

In the city where reggae rhythms echoed resilience, Marley moved through her daily routine with a determination that bordered on stoicism. Little did she know that the chapters of her life were about to unfold in unexpected ways, revealing the power of embracing vulnerability and challenging societal expectations. The journey into the bloom of Marley's life had only just begun.

The rhythmic hum of Kingston's urban pulse echoed through Marley's morning routine. As she prepared breakfast for her children, the aroma of ackee and saltfish danced through the air. Malik, Aria, and

Liam gathered around the table, their faces painted with the innocence of youth, unaware of the nuanced changes their mother was navigating.

Marley's professional attire, meticulously chosen to exude confidence, concealed the night's unrest and the invisible weight she carried. Her mirror reflected a woman who, despite the weariness that lingered in her eyes, held a determination that refused to waver.

The marketing firm she led thrived under her guidance, and yet, the corridors whispered tales of a woman at the cusp of transformation. Marley's office, adorned with accolades and framed photographs capturing moments of familial joy, became a sanctuary where she masked her internal struggles.

The demands of her career, combined with the intricacies of motherhood, left little room for Marley to acknowledge the subtle metamorphosis within. Her evenings were a symphony of homework, laughter, and the occasional reggae beats that wafted in from the lively streets outside.

As the clock ticked into the late hours, Marley's sanctuary shifted. The bedroom, once a haven of rest, became a battleground where sleep eluded her grasp. Night after night, she wrestled with the discomfort of hot flashes and the restlessness that accompanied hormonal shifts. In the soft glow of moonlight, Marley grappled with the silent struggle, determined not to let the world glimpse her vulnerability.￼

The weekends, once reserved for family outings and relaxation, now bore witness to Marley's silent battles. She found herself withdrawing from the gatherings with friends, concealing the occasional mood swings behind a smile that had weathered many storms.

The cityscape, with its vibrant colors and lively beats, felt both comforting and isolating. Marley's strength, a beacon admired by many, became a fortress that held her captive. The very resilience that defined her now stood as a barrier, preventing her from seeking solace in the company of those who cared.

The chapter of Marley's life titled "A Woman in Bloom" was unfolding, revealing the intricate layers beneath the vivacious exterior. Little did she know that the narrative, marked by career triumphs and familial joys, was poised for a profound evolution—one that would illuminate the power of vulnerability, connection, and the beauty inherent in the cycles of life. The journey had just begun, and Marley was on the brink of discovering the strength that lay in breaking the silence surrounding the unspoken aspects of womanhood.

Amidst the vibrant chaos of Kingston's streets, Marley found herself at the crossroads of her own narrative. The weight of her unspoken struggles intensified as work obligations demanded more of her attention, and the ever-growing independence of her children added new layers of complexity to her role as a mother.

The marketing firm, a domain where Marley once effortlessly commanded respect, now felt like a battleground where each decision carried the invisible burden of hormonal turmoil. The creative pitches she once crafted with unwavering focus were now occasionally marred by a mind clouded with the fog of fatigue. The undercurrents of uncertainty flowed beneath her professional façade, threatening the very foundation she had meticulously built.

At home, the twins were beginning to sense a subtle shift in their mother's demeanor. Aria, perceptive beyond her years, noticed the moments when Marley retreated into solitude, the invisible armor momentarily faltering. Liam, a beacon of exuberance, began to seek reassurance from the woman who had always been his unwavering source of strength.

Week after week, Marley found herself navigating a maze of emotions, wrestling with the dichotomy of a powerful career woman and a mother grappling with her internal landscape. The reggae beats that once synchronized with the cadence of her life now seemed to underscore the rhythm of change—a change she hesitated to acknowledge.

CHAPTER 2

Years before, when Malik was just a teenager and the twins mere toddlers, Marley confronted a health crisis that tested her resolve. A diagnosis, delivered with the weight of uncertainty, threatened to upend the stability she had painstakingly built. It was a battle that unfolded in sterile hospital rooms and echoed through sleepless nights.

Marley's determination emerged as a guiding force during those tumultuous days. With unwavering resilience, she navigated treatments, embraced uncertainties, and emerged triumphant against the odds. The victory, however, came at a cost—physical scars and emotional resilience earned through adversity.

As the years passed and health regained its steady rhythm, Marley tucked the memories of that battle away. It became a silent well of strength, a source of resilience that lay dormant until a new challenge presented itself—menopause.

The symptoms emerged gradually, disrupting the harmony Marley had cultivated in her personal and professional life. The relentless night sweats and the unpredictable mood swings were reminders of her body's evolution, whispers of change she had yet to confront.

Marley found herself at the crossroads once again. Yet, the lessons from her past battles were not lost on her. The quiet courage that propelled her through the earlier storm stirred within her.

It was during a crucial presentation at the marketing firm that the threads of Marley's facade began to unravel. The boardroom, usually a space where her confidence reigned supreme, became a battleground where hormonal fluctuations waged war against her composure.

As Marley addressed the team, a sudden wave of heat engulfed her, turning her face crimson. The beads of sweat forming on her forehead mirrored the intensity of her internal struggle. Words that once flowed effortlessly now stumbled over the edges of her consciousness, and the eyes of her colleagues registered a subtle shift—a deviation from the poised woman they had known. ￼The discomfort persisted, intensifying as the minutes ticked by. The once pristine boardroom became a stage where Marley grappled with a force beyond her control. She excused herself, leaving a trail of hushed whispers in her wake.

The moment Marley excused herself from the boardroom was marked by a symphony of whispers that lingered in the wake of her departure. Hushed conversations ensued among her colleagues, their speculations weaving a narrative of uncertainty and curiosity. The once-confident leader had become an enigma, leaving behind a room tinged with an unspoken question—what was happening to Marley?

As she rushed to her office, the corridor seemed to elongate, each step a reminder of the internal struggle she could not escape. The door closed behind her, muffling the sounds of the outside world. Alone within the familiar confines of her workspace, Marley felt the weight of the day pressing against her.

The discomfort, triggered by hormonal fluctuations, lingered as a palpable presence. Marley paced her office, the once-familiar surroundings now imbued with an unfamiliar tension. The reflections in the windows became distorted by the beads of sweat forming on her forehead. The rhythmic ticking of the clock echoed the irregular cadence of her own heartbeat.

Seated at her desk, Marley sought solace in the silence, grappling with a sense of inadequacy that threatened to erode the foundations of her confidence. The invisible battle waged within her, each passing moment intensifying the turmoil. The minutes stretched into an eternity, and Marley, usually a master of composure, found herself on the brink of vulnerability.

The discomfort, both physical and emotional, seemed unending. As she questioned her own abilities and the resilience that had defined her throughout her life, the whispers of colleagues outside her office door became a haunting chorus, amplifying the vulnerability she sought to conceal.

In a moment of desperation, Marley reached for the framed photograph on her desk—a snapshot capturing a family outing beneath the Caribbean sun. The smiles frozen in time were a stark contrast to the internal tempest she faced. The photograph, usually a source of joy, became a mirror reflecting the disparity between the image she projected and the struggle that unfolded within. In the heat of the moment, she threw the photograph against the wall, shattering the glass frame completely. The once joyful image now lay scattered in a mosaic of shards, mirroring the fractures within Marley's composed exterior. In the deafening aftermath of the crash, the silence of her office amplified the weight of her actions.

The immediate rush of remorse enveloped Marley as she stared at the remnants of the photograph. Each shard held a reflection of a moment tainted by the turbulence within her—a family frozen in fragments.

Regret etched across her face, Marley sank into her chair, cradling her head in her hands. The internal storm, initially confined to hormonal fluctuations, now spilled over into the physical world. The once-pristine office, a haven of professionalism, bore witness to the visceral unraveling of a woman who had held her struggles in silence for far too long.

Amid the echoes of her frustration and the melancholy of broken memories, Marley's vulnerability took center stage. The distorted reflections in the remaining shards of glass seemed to mirror the complexities of her own identity—a woman who had weathered storms yet found herself confronting an unprecedented tempest.

In the aftermath of her impulsive act, the solitude of the office became a cocoon where Marley grappled not only with the consequences of her frustration but also with the tangled emotions that had led to this outburst. The photographs on the wall, once a testament to a life well-lived, now bore the weight of her internal struggle.

As she surveyed the wreckage, Marley's gaze fell upon the photograph's fragments—a poignant metaphor for the fragmented aspects of her own life. The realization dawned that her strength, though formidable, had its limits, and the vulnerability she fought to conceal had erupted in a symphony of broken glass.

CHAPTER 3

Weeks passed, and Marley continued to navigate the challenges of menopause in silence. The discomfort persisted, a relentless companion shadowing her every step. The decision to share her internal struggles remained suspended, held captive by the fortress of her own resilience.

As the day of the crucial presentation approached, the weight of expectation mingled with the undercurrents of hormonal fluctuations. Marley, usually a master of preparation, found her focus disrupted by an unwelcome visitor—brain fog. The once-crystal-clear thoughts now wavered in a foggy labyrinth, creating a disorienting mental landscape.

The morning of the presentation dawned, and anxiety, a newfound companion, entwined with the hormonal tempest. Marley, determined to push through, gathered her composure. The virtual meeting room became a stage, and the stakes were higher than ever.

As she began her presentation, the fog thickened. Words, carefully chosen in moments of clarity, now struggled to find coherent expression. The screen shared a glimpse into Marley's world—professionalism teetering on the edge of vulnerability. Colleagues, clients, and stakeholders watched as the formidable leader grappled with the invisible battle within.

Midway through the presentation, the fog intensified. Marley, fighting the internal tempest, faltered. The anxiety, once a subtle hum, crescendo into a symphony of chaos. The carefully crafted narrative slipped through her fingers, and in a moment of vulnerability, the screen went dark.

The virtual room, once filled with anticipation, now hung in silent suspense. Marley's heart raced as she attempted to reconnect; the echoes of her struggle now broadcast for all to witness. The seconds felt like an eternity, and in the void of technological disconnect,

Marley confronted not only the limitations of her body but also the stark reality of her silent battle.

When the connection was reestablished, the damage was done. The momentum lost, the message muddled, Marley felt the weight of her internal battle reflected in the eyes of her virtual audience. The realization hit that the struggle she fought to conceal had disrupted not only her personal narrative but also the professional trajectory she had meticulously built.

In the aftermath of the failed presentation, Marley retreated to her office. The echoes of disappointment reverberated, and the decision to share her journey, once restrained, seemed to claw at the edges of her consciousness.

Marley's disrupted presentation rippled through the corporate landscape, leaving in its wake a complex tapestry of consequences. The multimillion-dollar contract, once within grasp, slipped through the company's fingers like elusive sand.

Colleagues, initially supportive, found themselves caught between empathy and professional frustration. The whispers in the virtual corridors of the company mirrored a mix of concern, disappointment, and a subtle questioning of Marley's ability to lead in the face of such unexpected challenges.

The stakeholders, pivotal players in the contract negotiations, conveyed a measured disappointment. The impact of Marley's struggle reverberated beyond the confines of the virtual meeting room, reaching into the delicate intricacies of business relationships. Trust, a commodity that took years to build, now faced a formidable test.

As Marley navigated the ensuing days, the professional fallout mirrored the turbulence within her personal world. The company, once propelled by her strategic prowess, now found itself recalibrating in the wake of a missed opportunity. The resilience she had embodied became a focal point for introspection within the corporate hierarchy.

At home, the repercussions of Marley's disrupted presentation infiltrated the sanctuary she had sought to preserve. Aria and Liam, perceptive beyond their years, sensed a shift in their mother's energy.

The vibrant rhythms of family life, once an anchor of stability, now bore the subtle traces of an emotional tempest.

The evening following the presentation, as Marley gathered her children for dinner, the weight of disappointment lingered in the air. The twins, sensing an unspoken tension, exchanged glances with furrowed brows. Marley, wrestling with her own vulnerability, grappled with the decision to share the professional setback with her children.

In a moment of contemplation, as the aroma of Jamaican spices filled the kitchen, Marley chose to shield her children from the corporate complexities that infiltrated her world. The disappointment, she decided, was a burden she would carry alone. The fortress of silence, though strained, held firm in this familial haven.

As the days unfolded, the symptoms of menopause, rather than lessening, intensified in tandem with the emotional tumult. The relentless night sweats, the unpredictable mood swings—each symptom became a poignant reminder of the intricacies woven into the fabric of Marley's life.

The once-rhythmic dance of bedtime routines with Aria and Liam now carried an undercurrent of unspoken tension. The bedtime stories, once narrated with unwavering enthusiasm, now echoed against the backdrop of a mother navigating the complexities of womanhood.

The veranda, once a space of solace, witnessed Marley's moments of silent reflection. The remnants of the broken photograph, carefully stored in a box, became a poignant metaphor for the fragments of her own resilience. The decision to share her journey, suspended in the aftermath of the disrupted presentation, gained weight with each passing day.

As the Caribbean moon cast its gentle glow over Kingston, Marley confronted the duality of her existence—resilient leader by day, vulnerable woman by night. The fortress of silence, once a refuge, began to feel confining. The complexity of Marley's journey, poised between professional setbacks and personal reckonings, stood at the crossroads of revelation.

CHAPTER 4

As Marley grappled with the nuances of menopause, she found herself confronting not just the physical and emotional aspects but also the cultural tapestry that framed her journey. In the vibrant landscape of Jamaica, discussions about women's health, particularly menopause, were often veiled in silence, wrapped in layers of societal norms and historical taboos.

Growing up, Marley had gleaned a wealth of wisdom from her mother, yet the topic of menopause remained conspicuously absent from their conversations. The cultural currents that swept through their lives dictated a certain level of privacy surrounding women's health matters. It was not that Marley's mother intentionally withheld information; rather, it was a product of a cultural legacy where such topics were deemed deeply personal, not meant for public discourse.

The surprise Marley felt upon entering the realm of menopause was not just a personal revelation but a reflection of a broader trend within her community. Women, conditioned by societal expectations and cultural norms, often chose to navigate the complexities of menopause privately. The natural progression of life, while acknowledged, carried an unwritten agreement of discretion.

As Marley grappled with night sweats and mood swings, she began to question the silence that surrounded menopause. The lack of intergenerational communication, the dearth of shared experiences, created a void she had not anticipated. It wasn't just a gap in knowledge; it was a cultural current that had carried over generations, woven into the fabric of womanhood.

In this introspective moment, Marley uncovered not just the cultural nuances but also realized that there was a prevailing narrative among women in her community. The unspoken understanding seemed to be that menopausal symptoms were an inevitable part of life, a rite of passage that required endurance rather than exploration of remedies.

It dawned on Marley that the silence surrounding menopause wasn't solely rooted in cultural norms but also in a collective perception that these symptoms were just something women had to endure. The lack of discourse on potential alleviation methods, on acknowledging that there might be ways to make this transition more manageable, struck a chord within her.

As the head of the marketing firm, Marley found herself at the nexus of professional responsibility and personal revelation. The echoes of her disrupted presentation reverberated not only through her personal life but also within the confines of her professional realm. The question of whether to address menopause in the workplace, particularly for the women under her leadership, now occupied a prominent space in her considerations.

In the weeks following the presentation, Marley began to contemplate the creation of a supportive environment for women experiencing menopause within her company. The realization that women's health, including menopause, was often overlooked in corporate settings prompted her to envision a workplace where discussions about these natural life transitions were not only welcomed but actively supported.

While Marley had not yet revealed her own struggle, the seeds of change had been planted. She envisaged workshops, support networks, and resources tailored to address the unique challenges women faced during menopause. The aim was not only to destigmatize the conversation but also to empower women with knowledge about managing their symptoms and navigating this phase of life with grace. [OBJ]

In this pivotal chapter of her professional journey, Marley recognized that fostering an open dialogue about women's health could contribute to a more inclusive and supportive workplace culture. The revelation of her own experience would not only be a personal disclosure but also a catalyst for broader change within the company.

As Marley contemplated the prospect of revealing her struggle with menopause to her co-workers, a complex tapestry of emotions and fears intertwined within her. The hesitation stemmed from a delicate dance between vulnerability and the expectations placed upon her as a leader.

One underlying fear was the concern of being perceived as less capable or less in control. The professional world, often characterized by a stoic facade, held expectations that leaders should navigate challenges with unwavering composure. Marley, acutely aware of the potential for judgment, grappled with the fear that her admission of vulnerability might be misconstrued as a sign of weakness.

Another fear stemmed from the societal stigma surrounding menopause. The silence that enveloped women's health matters, particularly menopause, had woven a narrative that these experiences should remain private. Marley, influenced by cultural nuances and professional expectations, worried about breaking a silence that had been upheld for generations.

There was also a fear of the unknown—the unpredictable ways in which her revelation might be received. Marley, accustomed to steering the ship with strategic precision, hesitated at the thought of relinquishing control over how her story would be perceived. The vulnerability that came with sharing such a personal aspect of her life left her standing at the edge of uncertainty.

Despite the hesitations and fears, a growing realization nudged at Marley's consciousness. The strength she had demonstrated throughout her career was not diminished by acknowledging her struggles; rather, it was magnified by the authenticity of her journey. The decision to reveal her menopausal experience wasn't just a personal revelation; it was a step towards reshaping cultural norms and fostering a more inclusive workplace.

CHAPTER 5

In the heart of Kingston, Jamaica, where the vibrant hues of bougainvillea dance against the azure skies and the rhythmic beats of reggae pulse through the air, Marley found solace amidst the breathtaking tapestry of her homeland.

As she navigated the complexities of her own journey, Marley took solace in the gentle breezes that carried the scent of tropical blooms—a symphony of fragrances that mirrored the diverse hues of her own emotions. The lush landscapes, adorned with the vivid colors of hibiscus and the majestic fronds of palm trees, stood as a testament to the resilience and beauty inherent in the Jamaican spirit.

The streets of Kingston, alive with the cadence of daily life, reflected the intricate threads woven into the cultural fabric of Jamaica. From the vibrant markets where fruits spilled over in a riot of colors to the soulful melodies echoing from reggae music joints, Marley immersed herself in the rich heritage that shaped her identity.

In the midst of her own narrative, Marley found inspiration in the warm embrace of the Caribbean sun, casting golden hues over the hills of Blue Mountains. The iridescent waters of Dunn's River Falls, reminiscent of liquid jewels, mirrored the resilience she sought to embody in the face of her unspoken struggles.

The culinary delights of Jamaica, with their fusion of flavors and spices, became a metaphor for the diverse elements interwoven into Marley's personal and professional life. Ackee and saltfish, jerk chicken, and the warmth of a cup of Blue Mountain coffee—all held the essence of a journey as intricate and flavorful as the dishes themselves.

In the passing weeks, Marley's struggle with the relentless symptoms of menopause cast a shadow over her daily life. Seeking solace, she ventured to her general practitioner, hoping for answers that would lift the veil of discomfort. However, the encounter proved to be a mere echo in the vast landscape of her unspoken journey.

The doctor's diagnosis, attributing her symptoms to stress, left Marley grappling with a sense of frustration. The hot flashes, each accompanied by an unwelcome surge of anxiety, continued to disrupt her nights, leaving her in a restless pursuit of elusive sleep.

The brain fog, a relentless companion, obscured the once-sharp edges of her thoughts. In the boardroom, where precision was paramount, Marley found herself navigating a mental labyrinth, each decision shrouded in the foggy veil of cognitive struggle.

The impact on her personal life became palpable. The once-vibrant rhythm of Marley's social existence seemed muffled, overshadowed by the embarrassment that accompanied each hot flash. The prospect of a date, once an exciting venture, now felt ensnared in the unpredictable dance of menopausal symptoms.

As Marley stood at the intersection of her professional and personal realms, the weight of unaddressed symptoms pressed upon her shoulders. The doctor's dismissal of her struggles echoed in her mind, leaving her torn between the acknowledgment of her symptoms and the desire to maintain an unwavering façade.

Marley delved into the labyrinth of her memories, a tapestry of her teenage years unfolded—a time when the whispers of menopause were woven into the very fabric of her family and community. The fragments of her past, once scattered in the recesses of her mind, began to coalesce into a mosaic of recognition. <OBJ>

She recalled the subtle but consistent shifts in her mother's demeanor, the echoes of arguments that seemed to dance through the corridors of their home like shadows. The bittersweet memories of Kingston Baptist Church emerged, adorned with the grace of women, including her mother, who wielded delicate paper fans as both accessory and necessity.

In those bygone days, Marley had perceived these ladies as paragons of grace and fashion, their fans a mere embellishment to their elegance. Now, with the wisdom of lived experience, she recognized the fan as a silent ally—a dignified defense against the relentless heat of hot flashes that had, in all likelihood, visited each of those women.

As the mosaic of memories unfolded, Marley's retrospective gaze extended beyond her mother to the collective experiences of women within the Kingston Baptist Church community. The communal whispers of shared struggles, the unspoken camaraderie within the swaying of fans, painted a portrait of women navigating the uncharted winds of menopause.

The echoes of recognition led Marley to a profound realization—that the journey she now trod had been paved, albeit silently, by the resilient footsteps of the women who had come before her. The memories of her mother, the shared glances among the ladies in church, whispered a narrative of silent strength and unspoken sisterhood.

CHAPTER 6

As time flowed like the meandering rivers that framed the edges of Jamaica, Marley found herself immersed in the ebb and flow of menopausal symptoms that showed no sign of abating. The small irritations had grown into formidable challenges, each day carrying a new set of discomforts that tested her resilience.

Determined to find solace in the absence of extensive resources on the island, Marley embarked on a journey of self-research. The vast landscape of the internet became her ally as she sought products, remedies, and advice that could offer respite from the relentless onslaught of symptoms.

In the intimate spaces of her home, Marley experimented with products she sourced from various corners of the digital world— cooling pads for the night sweats, herbal supplements for mood swings, and fabrics designed to combat the discomfort of hot flashes.

The limitations of resources on the island compelled her to become not only the protagonist of her journey but also the architect of her own relief.

Jamaica's small size and limited accessibility to specialized menopausal resources became apparent as Marley navigated this uncharted terrain. The sense of isolation, both geographically and in the realm of available support, underscored the need for a more widespread acknowledgment of women's health concerns on the island.

Yet, within these limitations, Marley's resilience shone brightly. The products she discovered, the remedies she explored, became not just solutions to immediate challenges but beacons of empowerment.

Within the pulsating rhythm of corporate life, Marley found herself ensnared in a different drama—one that would cast shadows over her career like a sudden eclipse. The incident unfolded during a critical negotiation, where the stakes were high, and the expectations even higher.

As Marley faced the negotiating table, the unrelenting heat of a hot flash surged through her, leaving her grappling with discomfort and anxiety. The carefully crafted arguments she had prepared became elusive in the haze of menopausal symptoms. Words stumbled, and clarity slipped away like grains of sand through her fingers.

The atmosphere in the boardroom shifted, the tension palpable as her counterparts exchanged knowing glances. Marley asked to be excused, unable to complete her presentation. Feeling embarrassed and defeated she rushed to the seclusion of her office.

News of the fumbled negotiation reached the higher echelons of the company, echoing through the corridors of power. The repercussions were swift and severe. Whispers of doubt that now threatened to overshadow Marley's years of dedication and strategic brilliance.

The aftermath of the negotiation debacle sent shockwaves through the company, placing Marley in the unenviable position of defending not just her actions but her entire career. Whispers of doubt echoed in the hallways, and the once unassailable leader found herself teetering on the precipice of professional uncertainty.

Amid the shadows cast by the incident, Marley grappled with a decision that carried weight beyond the confines of the boardroom. The stigma surrounding menopause, like an invisible adversary, threatened to obscure the reality of her struggle. The silence she had maintained to shield herself from judgment now became a barrier to understanding.

CHAPTER 7

In the quietude of her home, Marley weighed the cost of silence against the potential for understanding. The specter of the recent incident lingered, threatening not only her professional standing but the very foundation of the legacy she had built. A decisive choice loomed—one that would define not only her personal journey through menopause but also the future landscape of women's health awareness within the corporate sphere.

As the dawn of a new day painted streaks of gold across the Jamaican sky, Marley resolved to call a board meeting—an assembly of the minds that held the keys to her professional destiny. The prospect of laying bare her intimate struggles, of revealing the intricacies of menopause, carried a weight that transcended the confines of the boardroom.

With a steady voice that mirrored the resilience that had propelled her career, Marley stood before the board. In measured words, she unfolded the chapters of her menopausal journey—the sleepless nights, the anxiety-laden hot flashes, and the brain fog that had momentarily eclipsed her strategic brilliance.

Her intent was clear—to dispel the shadows of misunderstanding that had encroached upon her professional standing. Marley emphasized that menopause was not an ailment but a natural phase of life, a passage that countless women navigate with grace and resilience. She sought not pity but understanding, not sympathy but acknowledgment of the shared experiences that, until now, had been shrouded in silence.

In the hallowed chamber of the boardroom, Marley took a deep breath, the weight of her revelation heavy in the air. The tension, like an overture building to a crescendo, seized the room as she began to unveil the intimate layers of her menopausal journey.

Her words echoed with vulnerability, each sentence a poignant note in the symphony of disclosure. A few faces registered understanding, the silent acknowledgment of shared experiences. Yet, within the audience of power and ambition, the resonance of her revelation fell on ears that seemed deaf to empathy.

As Marley spoke of hot flashes disrupting negotiations, of the brain fog that had momentarily clouded her strategic brilliance, a dissonance emerged among the board members. Whispers of disbelief intertwined with sidelong glances, casting shadows of skepticism over her candid narrative.

The drama unfolded not only in Marley's revelation but in the reactions that rippled through the room. A few women, perhaps having faced similar battles in silence, nodded in silent empathy. Yet, the majority remained entrenched in the competitive currents that defined the corporate landscape. Ambition and opportunism, like undertones in a complex melody, threatened to drown out the vulnerability Marley had bared.

In the aftermath of her revelation, a palpable shift occurred—one that wasn't uniformly embracing. The dissonance among the board members transformed into a symphony of contrasting attitudes. Some viewed Marley's disclosure with empathy, recognizing the human behind the title. However, others, fueled by professional rivalry and the unforgiving nature of corporate dynamics, saw an opportunity in her vulnerability.

The aftermath of Marley's dramatic revelation plunged her into a corporate battlefield, where the discordant notes of ambition clashed with the vulnerability, she had bravely laid bare. The symphony of change, far from a seamless transition, unfolded as a gradual and arduous transformation. 🖾

As the days turned into weeks, Marley faced a landscape fraught with challenges. Some members of the board, moved by empathy and an understanding of women's health, stood by her side. Yet, a faction, driven by opportunism and a ruthless pursuit of power, sought to capitalize on the perceived weakness that had been unveiled.

The battle played out not only in the boardroom but in the subtle dynamics that shaped daily interactions within the company. Whispers of dissent and subtle maneuvers threatened to undermine Marley's authority. The vulnerability she had exposed became both a weapon wielded by adversaries and a rallying cry for those who sought a more empathetic corporate culture.

Amidst the tumult, Marley, with the resilience that had defined her career, decided that it was time to begin a gradual campaign for change. Her decision to fight for change marked the initial beat in the symphony of transformation.

CHAPTER 8

Recognizing the need for thorough understanding, Marley delved into extensive research on menopause. Nights that were once filled with restlessness became dedicated to absorbing information from medical journals, expert opinions, and personal accounts.

Armed with a wealth of knowledge, Marley meticulously crafted presentations outlining the physiological aspects of menopause, its impact on mental health, and the challenges women face during this transition. She became a self-appointed advocate, determined to dispel myths and bring clarity to a topic shrouded in misconceptions.

Marley's journey of self-education not only equipped her with the facts but also ignited a passion to bridge the knowledge gap within her organization. The conviction in her voice and the authenticity of her experiences transformed her into a compelling advocate for change.

It wasn't easy, Marley encountered resistance from an influential adversary, Alexander Grant, a charismatic but traditionalist executive. Alexander staunchly believed that corporate boardrooms were not suitable for women. Fueling his opposition, he rallied like-minded colleagues, influential figures who echoed Alexander's views.

Alexander, with his persuasive demeanor, used menopause as a weapon to undermine Marley's credibility and challenge her position. His calculated maneuvers aimed to paint women as unsuitable for leadership roles, injecting palpable tension into the narrative.

As the conflict intensified, Marley found herself entangled in a battle that extended beyond menopause awareness. The corporate landscape became the backdrop for a riveting story, where Marley's resilience faced the formidable resistance of Alexander and his collaborators, adding layers of tension and intrigue to the unfolding narrative.

Alexander employed subtle yet impactful tactics to undermine Marley's position on menopause. He strategically circulated misleading information within the organization, questioning the legitimacy of menopause as a significant workplace concern.

Using his influential network, he spread rumors suggesting that Marley's advocacy for menopause awareness was a personal agenda, aimed at gaining sympathy rather than addressing a genuine workplace issue. The duo strategically downplayed the importance of menopause education during team meetings, casting doubt on the necessity of such initiatives.

In more private settings, Alexander engaged in subtle acts of exclusion. Deliberately omitted Marley from crucial decision-making conversations, creating an atmosphere where her opinions were overlooked. He subtly implied that her focus on menopause was a distraction from the "real" priorities of the workplace.

These calculated efforts aimed to erode Marley's credibility and portray her as out of touch with the organization's objectives. The challenge for Marley was not just combating misinformation but also navigating the delicate balance of addressing the resistance without escalating tensions within the office.

The subtle attacks from Alexander took a toll on Marley, causing a mix of frustration and emotional exhaustion. The misinformation campaign stirred self-doubt, and the sense of isolation fueled moments of vulnerability. The exclusion from critical discussions further amplified the emotional weight Marley carried.

However, rather than breaking her down, these challenges fueled a deeper sense of determination within Marley. The adversity she faced became a driving force, igniting a stronger commitment to her mission. The mental and emotional toll served as a catalyst for Marley to refine her communication strategies, seeking more inclusive avenues to convey the importance of menopause awareness.

Marley, recognizing the need for resilience, channeled the emotional strain into a source of strength. The adversity became a transformative experience, solidifying her resolve to break down barriers and foster understanding. The challenges she encountered ultimately shaped the next steps in her journey, propelling her forward with a renewed sense

of purpose and determination.

CHAPTER 9

Marley adopted a multi-faceted approach to win against her adversaries. First, she meticulously gathered empirical evidence and testimonials from other employees, both men and women, who had experienced the impact of menopause and andropause in the workplace. These real-life stories served as powerful anecdotes to counteract the misinformation spread by Alexander and Jonathan.

To address their skepticism, Marley organized expert-led workshops on the physiological and psychological aspects of menopause. Bringing in professionals from relevant fields provided authoritative voices that substantiated the legitimacy of menopause as a workplace concern.

Understanding the power of personal narratives, Marley courageously shared her own experiences during a pivotal workshop. Her vulnerability, coupled with the factual information presented, resonated with her colleagues. The emotional connection created during this moment played a significant role in dismantling their resistance.

In addition, Marley initiated one-on-one conversations with Alexander, offering him a platform to express their concerns and engage in open dialogue. This personalized approach allowed her to address their misconceptions directly and provide them with the opportunity to ask questions in a supportive environment.

Through these comprehensive efforts, Marley gradually dismantled the walls of resistance. Alexander, confronted with irrefutable evidence, personal stories, and a more nuanced understanding, eventually became allies in Marley's mission. The victory was not only about convincing them of menopause issues' legitimacy but also about fostering a broader cultural shift within the corporate world.

Marley's partnership with Alexander proved transformative for the company. United by a shared commitment to fostering a more inclusive workplace, they collaboratively initiated a company-wide initiative aimed to break down barriers surrounding various aspects of diversity, with a particular focus on gender-related issues, including menopause.

Together, Marley and Alexander spearheaded workshops, training sessions, and awareness campaigns. They worked closely with HR to implement policies that supported employees navigating life transitions, including menopause. The company underwent a cultural shift, with a renewed emphasis on empathy, understanding, and a commitment to creating an environment where everyone felt valued.

As a symbol of their joint commitment, Marley and Alexander established a foundation dedicated to supporting initiatives promoting diversity, equity, and inclusion within and beyond the workplace. The fund sponsored community programs, educational events, and partnerships with organizations sharing their vision.

Associations with external organizations and thought leaders further amplified the impact of their efforts. The company's reputation flourished as it became recognized for its progressive stance on workplace inclusivity.

Marley and Alexander's collaboration became a beacon, inspiring other corporations to reevaluate their approaches. The company, once divided by resistance, emerged as a trailblazer, illustrating the profound positive transformations achievable when leaders unite for a common cause.

CHAPTER 10

As Marley sat on her veranda, overlooking the breathtaking Jamaican night, a symphony of sensations enveloped her. The cool breeze carried whispers of tropical blooms, their fragrances dancing through the air. The rhythmic hum of crickets provided a soothing soundtrack, harmonizing with distant reggae beats echoing from lively streets.

Above, a celestial masterpiece unfolded in the night sky. The moon, a radiant orb, cast its silvery glow over the landscape. Stars, like precious gems, sparkled in a cosmic dance, creating a celestial tapestry that stretched infinitely above Marley's veranda.

The veranda, adorned with vibrant bougainvillea, became a sanctuary bathed in moonlight. The foliage cast playful shadows, and the night embraced Marley with a tranquil energy. The city's vibrant colors, though subdued at night, still peeked through, adding to the enchantment of the scene.

Marley, amidst this natural and celestial beauty, reflected on her accomplishments. The veranda, a witness to her struggles and victories, became a space for quiet contemplation. The sense of fulfillment and pride mingled with the night air, creating an atmosphere of gratitude and serenity.

As the cool breeze wrapped around her, Marley's gaze wandered to the stars, each one celebrating the journey she had undertaken. In this picturesque Jamaican night, the veranda became a haven where the beauty of accomplishment merged seamlessly with the natural wonders surrounding her.

As Marley sat on her veranda, the weight of the past year's journey settled on her contemplative shoulders. The tropical night, with its gentle breeze and moonlit glow, provided a reflective backdrop to her thoughts.

In the stillness, Marley's mind rewound through the challenges and triumphs that defined her path. The sacrifices she made echoed in the rustling leaves, reminders of moments missed with her children. The nights spent immersed in research and advocacy seemed to intertwine with the nocturnal melodies of Kingston.

Her children were the driving force behind her tireless efforts. Her love for them fueled the determination that carried her through. Yet, Marley could not escape the occasional pang of guilt for the times she missed being fully present with them.

The veranda, bathed in the soft glow of moonlight, became a space where Marley reconciled the sacrifices with the greater purpose. The symphony of crickets echoed her inner reflections, acknowledging the trials and acknowledging the strength it took to persevere. As she retired to her bed, she felt at peace.